Arthur and the
Best Coach Ever

A Marc Brown Chapter Book

Arthur and the Best Coach Ever

Text by Stephen Krensky

Little, Brown and Company

Boston   New York   London

First Edition

The characters and events portrayed in this book are fictitious. Any
similarity to real persons, living or dead, is coincidental and not intended
by the author.

Arthur® is a registered trademark of Marc Brown.

Text has been reviewed and assigned a reading level by Laurel S. Ernst,
M.A., Teachers College, Columbia University, New York, New York;
reading specialist, Chappaqua, New York.

Library of Congress Cataloging-in-Publication Data

Krensky, Stephen.
    Arthur and the best coach ever / text by Stephen Krensky. — 1st ed.
    p. cm. — (A Marc Brown Arthur good sports chapter book ; bk. 4)
    Summary: When Arthur's soccer team gets a new coach who gives them
brand-new uniforms and lots of ice cream, it takes them a while to realize
that he doesn't know how to coach soccer.
    ISBN 0-316-12216-5
    [1. Soccer — Fiction. 2. Coaching (Athletics) — Fiction. 3. Coaches
(Athletics) — Fiction. 4. Animals — Fiction.] I. Title.

PZ7.K883 Ak 2001
[Fic] — dc21   2001029107

10 9 8 7 6 5 4 3 2 1

LAKE (hc)
COM-MO (pb)

Printed in the United States of America

For Tucker Eliot Brown

Chapter 1

. . . .

"Sounds goofy," said Buster. "Explain it again."

He and Arthur were standing on the school playground. It was late Saturday morning, and they had ridden their bikes over to kick around a soccer ball.

Arthur sighed. "One more time," he said. "To do a bicycle kick, you lie down on your back and kick the ball backward over your head."

"Okay, okay," said Buster. "I can't do it, but I can see it. Why do they call it a bicycle kick?"

"I guess because you kind of move your legs like you're pedaling."

Buster shook his head. "Even so, nobody pedals upside down on his back. They should have called it something else."

"Like what?"

"I don't know," said Buster. "Maybe a topsy-turvy kick or an upside-down kick. Bicycle just seems wrong somehow."

"Well, it wasn't my idea," Arthur replied. "I have enough trouble in soccer just keeping the ball in bounds."

"Oh, I'm sure you'll do better this year. We all will."

Arthur nodded. Last year the Lakewood Lightning had gone through what Coach Murphy called a "rebuilding season." They had won only two games, and even those two had gone down to the wire. But the coach had reminded them that they were a young team. "Next year" they would get a chance to shine.

And, as Buster pointed out, next year had arrived.

"Hey, guys!" said Muffy, calling out from across the field.

She ran over to them. "Have you heard the news?"

They shook their heads.

"I hope this isn't about some weekend homework," said Buster.

"It's not about school," said Muffy. "It's about soccer."

Arthur and Buster said they hadn't heard anything.

Muffy smiled. "Good. Then I get to tell you. Coach Murphy won't be coaching this year. He couldn't fit it into his schedule anymore."

"Not even part-time?" said Buster.

Muffy shook her head.

"That's too bad," said Arthur. "He was a good coach."

"Yeah," said Buster. "He never yelled at

me, even when I almost deserved it." Buster paused. "So I guess we'll get a new coach. Whoever it is, I hope he doesn't use a whistle the way Mr. Ratburn does at recess. That gives me a headache."

"Hmmm," said Arthur. "You don't suppose Mr. Ratburn would —"

"It's not Mr. Ratburn," said Muffy. "I know who it is."

"Don't just stand there," said Buster. "Tell us."

"I'll give you a hint. We're all getting new uniforms and a new name."

"New uniforms?" said Buster. "Not just T-shirts?"

"That's right. Shirts, shorts, socks. The whole outfit."

Arthur scratched his head. "What was wrong with Lakewood Lightning? I always thought the name made me run faster."

"Times change, Arthur," said Muffy. "You have to go with the flow."

"And which flow is that?" asked Arthur.

"The Crosswire Comets!"

Buster laughed. "That's a joke, right?"

"No," Muffy insisted. "That's the name."

"Who would name the team after you?" said Buster. "I mean, it's not like you're the best play— oh . . ."

"That's right," Muffy said, folding her arms. "My father's the new coach. Isn't that great?"

Arthur and Buster weren't sure what to say.

Chapter 2

• • • • • • • • • • • •

"Hello, everyone," said the big man standing at the edge of the soccer field. "For most of you, I need no introduction. I'm sure you've seen my ads on TV. Still, just to be on the safe side, let me say that I'm Ed Crosswire, president of Crosswire Motors."

Muffy clapped loudly.

"Now, I know that all of you were expecting Coach Murphy to be back this year. So was I. But he found himself with too many other commitments. That left us without a coach, and I was asked to step in."

Muffy clapped again.

"Is she going to do that after every sentence?" Buster whispered to the Brain.

The Brain shook his head. "I'm sure her hands will get tired eventually."

Coach Crosswire put his hands on his hips. "Now, I know this all came about rather suddenly, but I'm sure we can make everything work out. And I wanted to get off on the right foot, this being soccer and all. So I've brought along new uniforms in assorted sizes."

"Uniforms?" said Francine. "Real uniforms?"

The coach nodded. "I wouldn't put a car on the road that didn't look its very best. And I want the Crosswire Comets to feel the same way. My daughter, Muffy, picked out the colors."

"That explains the pink stripes," Buster whispered to Arthur.

"Also," Coach Crosswire went on, "I

8

know you'll be working hard at games and practices, so afterward there will always be ice cream for everyone."

Binky's eyes opened wide. "Ice cream?" he said.

"That's right," said Coach Crosswire.

"After every practice and every game?"

"Right again."

Binky beamed. "Way to go, Coach!"

Coach Crosswire folded his arms. "Thank you. So, let's get started. In my business, you have to know how to handle a customer. In soccer, you have to know how to handle the other team. To do that, we need to practice. Um, I'm sure you had a routine down with Coach Murphy, so let's begin with that. Meanwhile, I'll walk around and get a sense of how everyone is doing."

The kids broke into small groups and began passing the ball back and forth.

As the coach passed Buster heading a ball, he jumped in with a comment.

"Now, remember to put your hands up, Buster. You don't want to —"

"But why, Coach, since we can't use our hands in soccer?"

"Right, right. Yes . . . of course. But hand placement is important. You have to maintain a proper balance."

"Oh. Okay."

Off to one side, Arthur and Francine were lining up a couple of balls.

"Coach, could you help me with my corner kick?" asked Arthur.

"Corner kick?"

"Yeah, I need to get it to lift more."

"Hmmm. . . . Maybe later, Arthur. I've got a little more organizing to do first. You practice on your own. I'm sure you'll make progress."

"Um, okay."

As the coach moved on, Arthur stared at the ground.

"What's the matter?" asked Francine.

"He doesn't think I can do it."

"Who?" said Francine. "What?"

"Muffy's father," Arthur said. "Coach Murphy probably told him I wasn't any good at corner kicks. So he doesn't want to waste his time on me."

"I don't know, Arthur. He might just be busy."

Somehow that didn't make Arthur feel any better.

Chapter 3

· · · · · · · · · · ·

"Arthur, pass the broccoli," said his father.

The whole family was sitting around the dinner table. D.W. was telling a story about how someone in art class had eaten all the paste in the big jar.

"But nobody knows who did it," she said. "It's a mystery."

"Look for somebody who forgot to bring his lunch," said Mr. Read. "Arthur, did you hear me?"

"Huh?" Arthur blinked. "Oh, the broccoli . . ."

He picked up the bowl.

D.W. laughed. "He's probably imagining himself in his fancy new uniform. Or thinking about all that ice cream."

Baby Kate got very excited and started pounding her high-chair tray.

"See what you've started, D.W.?" said Mrs. Read. "No, Kate, no ice cream now. Maybe later."

"What's this about uniforms and ice cream?" asked Mr. Read. "It isn't exactly your classic combination."

"It's no big deal," said Arthur.

"Is too!" said D.W. "Muffy's dad is Arthur's new soccer coach. He got them new uniforms and promised them lots of ice cream. They're the Crosswire Comets."

"That certainly has a commercial ring to it. Ed Crosswire has always had an ear for marketing."

"A comet's just a big, dirty snowball," said Arthur. "We learned about them in class."

"That's true," said his father. "But comets are also fast and powerful."

Arthur shrugged. "Lightning is fast and powerful, too."

His mother nodded. "We understand, Arthur. It's only natural that you should miss Coach Murphy. But I'm sure this change will work out fine."

"I guess. But Coach Murphy was good at giving me pointers."

The longest stretch limo Arthur had ever seen pulled up in front of the practice field.

"Look at that!" said Buster. "Is this how we're traveling to away games, Coach? It must be the biggest car in the world. I'll bet everyone can fit in there."

"Of course," said Coach Crosswire. "My team always travels first-class. Come on, step right up. And inside there's TV, CD, DVD, VCR. . . ."

"Wow!" said Binky. "The whole alphabet."

"And free juice dispensers," the coach added. "I had them put in special."

As the team started to file in, the coach pulled Arthur aside.

"I'm sorry, Arthur," he said, "but we really don't need you on this trip."

"But, Coach, I thought there was room for everybody. . . ."

"Oh, there's room, Arthur. It's just that we really don't need you. We need someone who can handle those corner kicks."

"But, Coach, I'm getting better. Really."

"I'm sure you are. Maybe next time."

As Arthur stood at the curb, the limo pulled away. He couldn't even tell if anyone waved good-bye, because all the kids were hidden behind tinted glass.

"He's doing it again," said D.W.

"I am not," said Arthur.

Mr. Read coughed. "You do look like you're a million miles away," he said.

"No, I'm right here. And I want to hear more about the mysterious paste robber."

D.W. stared at him. "You do? All right, who are you, and what have you done with my brother?"

"Very funny, D.W. Of course, if you'd rather not tell . . ."

"Okay, okay. Well, I do have a few ideas. . . ."

And she told them every single one and followed with her really big story — how Stinky the hamster had escaped after recess.

Chapter 4

• • • • • • • • • • •

The next day at school, everyone was still talking about the new coach.

"My uniform fits really well," said Francine. "Not too loose and not too tight."

"I wonder if we can order sundaes and floats," said Binky.

"Probably," said the Brain. "Coach Crosswire seems very thorough. And I know he placed a big order with my mom at the ice-cream shop."

"What do you think, Arthur?" asked Francine.

"Huh?"

"Aren't you listening? We're talking about the soccer team."

"Oh." Arthur blinked. "What about it?"

"Do you like all the changes?"

"Um, sure. I mean, who doesn't like ice cream? Of course . . . well . . . nothing."

Francine frowned. "Now, don't be a party pooper. There's no rule that says ice cream and soccer can't be connected."

Arthur had no answer for that.

At practice that afternoon, the kids were divided into two teams for a scrimmage.

"We've got three extra kids," Coach Crosswire explained. "So we'll have to rotate you in. Um, let's see. . . . Arthur, Sue Ellen, and George, you start off on the sideline with me. The rest of you count off and divide into two teams."

Arthur was disappointed not to start on the field, but he figured he would get his turn soon enough.

As play began, the ball was quickly passed down to one end. Muffy was standing in goal. As a kick was made, she barely moved.

"SCORE!" Francine yelled.

Buster, who was playing sweeper, stared at Muffy. "Why didn't you dive for the ball?" he asked.

Muffy glared at him. "This is a brand-new uniform."

"But you're the goalie. You're supposed to block shots," said Buster.

"Hellllll-o! Did I mention the new uniform? If I lunge for the ball, I'm going to end up in the dirt. And those kinds of stains never come out."

Arthur glanced at Coach Crosswire, to see if he would say anything to Muffy. But he was looking at some papers on his clipboard and didn't seem to notice.

A few minutes later, Sue Ellen and

George went in as substitutes. "You're next," the coach told Arthur.

Arthur watched as the Brain charged down the wing and crossed the ball over to Binky. But Binky wasn't paying attention, and the ball scooted past him. Fern, playing in goal, picked it up and gave it a boot.

"Binky, you have to concentrate," said the Brain, as Binky shuffled past him.

"Huh? What?"

"I said you have to concentrate. That was a perfect pass."

"I *am* concentrating," Binky insisted.

The Brain looked at him skeptically. "On what?" he asked.

"On the ice cream after practice. I'm trying to decide which flavors I want."

Arthur looked over at Coach Crosswire again. He was pacing back and forth. Arthur was surprised to see the coach so worked up over one play. Then he realized

the coach was talking on a cell phone. Arthur couldn't hear what he was saying, but the conversation clearly had his full attention.

Arthur waited and waited and waited. Surely the coach was going to put him in at some point.

Finally, Coach Crosswire hung up and looked around. "Oh, Arthur . . . still waiting. I suppose we should get you in there, shouldn't we?"

"Yes, please."

"All right. Oops, there's my phone again. Hold on for a minute."

And he took the incoming call, leaving Arthur standing on the sideline.

Chapter 5

● ● ● ● ● ● ● ● ● ● ●

That night after dinner, Muffy went to see her father in his study. He was talking on the phone.

"I expect those sedans to arrive Friday. Don't talk to me about thunderstorms. That's why they invented windshield wipers. You heard what I said. . . . That's better. . . . All right, get back to me when you hear something."

He hung up the phone. "Dolts! Chowderheads! If they think I'm going to be roadkill on the business highway, they'd better think again."

"Yeah, they'd better think again," said

Muffy, although she couldn't help wondering a little who *they* were.

Her father looked at her. "So, what can I do for you, Muffin?"

"Nothing," she said. "I'm just excited about the team. I mean, everyone's used to Francine's dad coaching baseball, but now you're just as involved as he is."

"Hmmph! Yes, well, soccer's the biggest sport in the world. Good to be a part of it."

"So, Daddy, what do you think of the team so far?"

"What do I think?"

Muffy nodded. "What do you think our chances are?"

Her father hesitated. "Well, it can be difficult to predict these things. I'm sure we'll either win games or lose them. And ties are always possible. Of course, winning will be better. Not that there's anything wrong with losing. You can't win them all."

"Do you think we'll run into any problems?" Muffy asked.

"You never know when you can hit a slow period. That's what rebates and incentives are for. Of course, some players are showroom specials. Others really belong on the back lot. And then there are the players who need new batteries. But I'm sure we can jump-start them back into action."

"It's just so exciting," said Muffy.

Muffy was sitting in a shiny, new convertible, next to her father. They were driving slowly down Main Street in Elwood City. The sidewalks were lined with people, all cheering and throwing confetti.

"You're the best!"

"We're so proud!"

"Way to go, Muffy!"

The rest of the team was riding in used cars behind Muffy. The whole parade was passing

under a banner announcing the team's unde-
feated season.

"I thank you!" Muffy called out. "We all
thank you."

When they reached the steps of Town Hall,
Muffy and her father were met by the mayor.

"We're giving you the key to the city," he
told Coach Crosswire.

"Will it fit any of my cars?" he asked.

Everyone laughed as the coach accepted his
award. Then the whole team gathered around
them.

"Three cheers for Muffy and her dad!" they
all shouted.

"Well, I've still got work to do," said her
father.

Muffy blinked. "It's really great that
you're doing this," she said.

"Are you having as much fun as when
we built that miniature castle for you in
the backyard?"

"The one with the little moat and baby alligators?" asked Muffy.

He nodded.

"Close," she said, smiling. "Very close."

Chapter 6

● ● ● ● ● ● ● ● ● ● ● ●

The first game of the season was always exciting, and most of the players arrived early to loosen up.

"I feel fast today," said Buster. "Like a snowball rolling —"

"A snowball?" said the Brain. "Since when are snowballs known for their blazing speed?"

"You didn't let me finish. Like a snowball rolling down the steepest mountain, rushing toward —"

"We get the point, Buster," said Arthur. "We'll make sure we stay out of your way."

"Can I have everyone's attention?" said Coach Crosswire, clapping his hands together. "This is our first game, and there's nothing to be nervous about. We can handle the Hurricanes. Just play the way that I know you can play while I watch you play that way."

"What does that mean?" Buster whispered to Francine.

She just shrugged.

As the two teams took their positions, Muffy went to her place on the right wing.

"I didn't know you played right wing," said the Brain. "You hate to run, and wings have to run all the time."

"You've forgotten one important thing," said Muffy. "Wings play closer to the sidelines. That makes it easier for everyone to see how nice I look in my new uniform."

Arthur was too far away to hear them, but he looked a bit confused. "Everything seems all mixed up," he said to himself.

"Binky's playing center forward even though he's strong on defense. And Francine, who has the best shot on the team, is playing stopper, which means she'll never get near the opposing goal."

Worst of all, as far as he was concerned, Arthur was stuck in goal. There was something very lonely about the goalie position that made Arthur feel uncomfortable. True, if he made a good play everyone would see it clearly, but if he messed up a goalie has no place to hide.

Arthur was also convinced that the coach had put him in goal as a way of getting rid of him. As long as the team played well, he might never be tested.

But he wasn't that lucky. The Hurricanes came out strong, pouring on the pressure and never letting up. Arthur dove to the left and he dove to the right. He leapt high and he scrambled low. None of it helped much. By the end of the first half, he felt like one of those metal ducks in an arcade, the kind that is always getting shot at.

It didn't help that Fern was on defense. Whenever the ball came near her, she froze in confusion. The next moment she always lost the ball to the opposing player.

When the game finally ended, the Comets had lost, 6–0.

Everyone looked a little discouraged, but Coach Crosswire gathered them for a few encouraging words. "That wasn't so bad," he began.

"It wasn't so good, either," muttered Binky.

"Now, don't worry," the coach went on. "It's only natural to have a few kinks to work out in a new model. But you'll see. . . . We'll have things running smoothly and driving down that highway to victory in no time."

Chapter 7

• • • • • • • • • • •

A week later the kids piled out of Mr. Ratburn's class when the last bell rang.

"I can't believe how much homework we have tonight," said Buster.

"It should be against the law to give homework at all," said Binky. "If I were president, it would be the first thing I would change."

"Don't forget, we have a soccer game," Francine reminded them.

Everyone groaned.

"I can't believe I'm saying this," said Sue Ellen, "but I'm starting to dislike ice cream."

"I'm not," said Buster. "But I don't like all of the changes this year. I get the feeling the coach isn't always paying attention. In that last game, I got tripped and hit my knee. I told him I should come out, but he waved me back. 'You've still got some life in your tires,' he said."

They changed into their uniforms and walked out to the playing field. Coach Crosswire was already there, and so was Muffy. They were unloading balls from the soccer bag.

Francine ran over to help. "Any special tips today, Coach?" Francine asked.

"We will win," said Coach Crosswire, "if we score more goals than the other team."

"Oh."

He walked over to meet the referee, leaving Francine and Muffy alone.

"What did you mean by that?" Muffy asked.

"What do *you* mean?" Francine answered.

"Francine Frensky, I know that tone. What's up?"

Francine shrugged. "I just wanted some extra practice. When my dad coaches baseball, he hits grounders to the infield and pop-ups to the outfield. He teaches us stuff."

"Everybody's different," Muffy insisted. "My dad's doing a great job, too. Kicking the ball around isn't the only important thing for a coach. There are lots of other things. It's not his fault we're losing games. He's not the one out on the field."

"I know that," Francine said. "But he does seem to try to do a lot of things at once."

"That's right," agreed Muffy. "And not everybody can manage that. You're just —" She was interrupted by the referee's whistle calling for the start of the game.

As play started, Arthur found himself on the sideline. He wanted to ask which position he would be playing, but the coach was busy. A parent from the opposing team who had bought a car at Crosswire Motors had come over to say hello.

Muffy didn't see this. The ball had unexpectedly bounced her way, and she was charging down the wing. She was still mad about what Francine had said and wanted to prove to her and everyone else that Crosswires did their part. Muffy faked to the outside, and when the opposing fullback slipped on the grass, she cut toward the goal — and fired!

SCORE!

Muffy stood frozen in shock. She had never scored before, and it was a very strange feeling. As the team gathered around to congratulate her, she looked over to her father.

He wasn't even looking her way. He was

still talking with his customer. Muffy's face fell. Her first goal, and her father the coach had missed it!

Maybe Francine was right, after all.

Chapter 8

• • • • • • • • • • •

"Daddy, we have to talk."

Muffy was standing in the doorway to her father's study. He was sitting in the big, leather chair behind his desk, swiveling back and forth.

"Sure, Muffster. Just let me make this one call."

"No, Daddy. Please. We need to talk *now.*"

Her father put down the phone. He knew *that* tone. Muffy only used it when her front end was way out of alignment.

"All right. What's up?" he said.

"Do you know what happened at the game today?"

"Of course. We lost. Again."

"True," said Muffy. "But did you notice who scored a goal?"

"Ah, let's see. Binky, Francine . . ."

"What about me?"

"You?" He looked surprised.

"That's right. The first goal of my entire career and you didn't even notice. You were too busy talking with that parent from the other team."

"He's one of my best customers. You know, Muffster, Crosswire Motors doesn't run itself," said Mr. Crosswire.

"I know, I know. You work really hard, and that's important. But the other kids say that you aren't really paying attention to them. I defended you. Now I think maybe they were right."

"The kids were talking about me?" asked her father.

Muffy nodded.

"And they're not happy?"

Muffy nodded again.

"I thought everyone would love the uniforms and ice cream," said Mr. Crosswire.

"They do. But, well, the team needs more than that. We need to learn stuff, too."

The doorbell rang.

"Oh," said Muffy. "That must be Arthur. I forgot he was coming over. We're working on a history project together."

"Well, that's good timing, if you ask me," said Mr. Crosswire. "Let's get him in here and see what he thinks."

"Dad, I'm not sure. . . ."

"Well, I am."

Muffy sighed and went to get Arthur. When she returned, Coach Crosswire smiled at Arthur.

"Ah, Arthur. Just the person we wanted to see. Muffy and I have been talking about the soccer team and how everything is working out. We thought we'd get your opinion, too."

Arthur looked uncomfortable. "Um, I don't think I'm a good one to ask."

"Why not?" asked the coach.

"Well, because you don't think I'm very good. You should ask someone better."

Coach Crosswire's mouth dropped open. "I don't think you're good? Of all the misfiring pistons. . . . Why would you say that?"

"You keep me on the sidelines a lot," Arthur explained. "And whenever I ask you for help, you always make an excuse or something. I figured you just thought I wasn't worth helping."

Coach Crosswire got very red in the face. "Oh, Arthur, that's not it at all." He rubbed his nose uncomfortably. "Can you keep a secret?"

Arthur nodded.

"The truth is," the coach said, lowering his voice, "I don't know much about soccer. When Coach Murphy called, I wanted to help out, so I agreed to take his place. But I didn't think it would be so complicated. In my day, soccer was just kicking the ball and seeing what happened next."

Arthur looked relieved. "So you don't think I'm terrible?"

"Not at all. When you first asked me about a corner kick, I just didn't know what it was. I guess I was hoping that if I left you on your own, you'd figure it out for yourself."

Arthur couldn't believe it. Maybe he wasn't really as bad as he thought.

"Um, so, Arthur, I hope now we've cleared things up."

"Oh, right," said Arthur.

"Good, good. I'm sorry to have steered you in the wrong direction. And Muffy, I'm sorry I missed your goal. I'm going to read up on a few soccer plays and see what I can do to help the team." Coach Crosswire wiped his forehead with a handkerchief. "I'm just glad we're back on the road and ready to roll."

Chapter 9

•••••••••••

When Coach Crosswire arrived at the next game, he got out of the car and started over to the field. His cell phone began to ring. He took it out of his pocket and stared at it. Then he put it back in the car.

Some members of the team were already warming up. Coach Crosswire went over to talk with Fern.

"Fern, I want to discuss a few things before today's game."

Fern looked up. "You do?"

"Yes, yes, I do." The coach cleared his throat. "I can't pretend to be an expert on soccer, but I do know a little about timing.

You have to wait for the right moment —
and then make the most of it."

"But I'm not good at soccer," Fern said
quietly. "That's the problem."

"Ah," said the coach, "that's what the
other team may think, too. And *that's* your
strength."

"It is?" said Fern.

"Absolutely. When you look scared, the
other team sees that. Naturally, they think
you *are* scared."

Fern shuddered. "And they're right."

"Never mind that. Picture what hap-
pens next. They move in on you —"

"To take the ball away."

"Exactly. But what if you didn't let
them do that?" said Coach Crosswire.

Fern sighed. "But, Coach, I'm not good
enough to dribble through them."

"That's okay. I, um, wouldn't be, either.
A station wagon doesn't have to compete

with a sports car. They each have their advantages. What if . . . what if once the other team moved in, once they committed themselves, you kicked the ball over their heads?"

"That's all?"

He nodded. "Just do that. If enough of them have rushed up, our forwards will be open."

Fern brightened. "I could do that, I think."

"Excellent," said Coach Crosswire. He moved among the other players, making comments along the way.

Their game was against the Hingham Hornets. Once it started, the Hornets swarmed forward, scoring two quick goals.

"Settle down, settle down," Coach Crosswire called encouragingly from the sideline. "We've seen their sting, but we've got plenty of time."

After that, the ball seesawed from end to end, but neither team got off a good shot. When the Hornets' defense knocked the ball out of bounds next to the goal-post, the referee called for a Comet corner kick.

"Arthur, take the kick," Coach Cross-wire yelled.

"Me, Coach?" said Arthur.

"You've been practicing, haven't you? Well, let's have a look. Now move it."

Arthur ran to the corner and took a deep breath. Francine, Sue Ellen, and Buster were moving around the goal, trying to stay free.

Arthur tried to remember everything he had learned about corner kicks. He kicked the ball, not with his toe but farther down his foot on the inside. The ball lifted over the heads of the defenders and landed in front of Buster, who was stationed at the far post.

The ball sailed through the air, landing right in front of Buster. He trapped it neatly and wound up for a kick.

SCORE!

"One to go!" shouted Buster.

But that one proved hard to get. Time was running out and Fern found herself with the ball. That old feeling came over her, and she knew she looked really scared. But as the Hornets closed in, she remembered what the coach had told her — and gave the ball a good kick.

The ball floated over the heads of the defense. Binky cut across from the wing to meet it and fired it toward the net.

GOAL!

"All tied up!" cried Muffy.

And that was how the game ended. As

the Comets gathered for a cheer, Arthur stepped up to the coach.

"Good work," he said.

Coach Crosswire smiled. "You, too," he said. "Maybe we're all getting the hang of this."

Chapter 10

• • • • • • • • • • • • •

"You look tired," said Arthur.

He was standing at Muffy's front door two days later. He had come over to work on their project.

She grunted back at him and yawned.

"Hey, I just wanted to tell you . . . everybody really likes the way your dad is coaching."

Muffy grunted again.

"I thought you'd be happy," said Arthur.

Muffy leaned on the door. "I'm too tired to be happy. My father got me out of bed at dawn this morning. Dawn! 'Just to kick the ball around,' he said." She sighed. "I think we've created a monster, Arthur. I even caught him watching one of those international games on TV."

"Well, practice was great yesterday. Your father's really getting into it."

"That's the problem. Now he wants me to try every position. He says he will help me realize my full potential."

"What's wrong with that?"

Muffy shook her head. "Arthur, I can keep my uniform clean in one position or maybe even two. But if I have to keep moving around, forget it."

Arthur laughed. "That's the way the ball bounces," he said. "Maybe you could think of it as a challenge."

Muffy yawned again. "Doing a project with *you* is challenge enough," she said.

"But I won't mess up any uniforms," Arthur pointed out.

"Thank goodness!" said Muffy, laughing, and she turned around to lead him into the house.